# ROSES

# ROSES

## PETER MURRAY
THE CHILD'S WORLD

In the 1800s, when a young man wished to date a young lady, he would first send her a single red rose. If the lady sent back a yellow rose, it meant she thought the young man was not serious. If she returned a plain green leaf, it meant she did not like him. If she replied with another red rose, it was an invitation for him to call on her.

For many centuries, the rose has symbolized love, romance, and beauty. According to legend, the Egyptian queen Cleopatra greeted her Roman admirer Marc Antony in a room filled two feet deep with rose petals! Today, one of the most popular romantic gifts is a dozen long-stemmed roses.

The rose is related to the strawberry, the apple, and the peach. Long before people were putting roses into vases and growing them in gardens, roses grew wild in Asia, Europe, and North America. Scientists have discovered fossil roses in rocks 40 million years old! Roses still grow wild in most places. You can find them in the woods, in ditches, in hedges, and in fields. Wild roses usually have only five petals, but they smell wonderful.

Roses are best known for their beautiful blossoms, but they also produce a fruit. When a rose's petals drop off, a small seed capsule is left behind. This is called the rose's *hip*. Rose hips contain the tiny fruits of the rose plant. Though they are too tart and hard to eat, rose hips are used to make tea and jelly. The hips of *Rosa rugosa* are so rich in vitamin C that drug manufacturers use them to make vitamin tablets.

Most of the roses we see in gardens today are *hybrids*. Hybrids form when the pollen from one type of rose fertilizes the seeds of a different type of rose, creating an entirely new variety. Gardeners have been creating hybrid roses since ancient times. There are now many thousands of varieties.

The most popular rose today is the *hybrid tea*, with its many colors, intense fragrance, long stems, and large blossoms. People grew the first hybrid teas more than 100 years ago. Most of the roses you see in florist shops are hybrid teas.

In Bulgaria and India, people use the fragrant Damask rose to make a scented oil called *attar of roses*. It takes 4,000 pounds of roses to make one pound of attar! Attar of roses is sold to perfume and toiletry manufacturers for more than $1,000 a pound! It is one of the most expensive substances on earth.

The finest French perfumes are made from the petals of the pink cabbage rose. The scent from thousands of rose petals goes into each tiny bottle of Chanel No. 5 and other famous perfumes.

Rosebushes come in every shape and size, from the stately tree rose to the sprawling, crawling, vinelike climbers.

Most garden roses are actually a combination of two different plants. The roots and lower stem are from a strong, hardy rose. A small bud from another rose, chosen for the type of blossom, is *grafted* to the root stock. The resulting bush combines the best features of both plants: a strong root system and beautiful flowers.

If you ever see a rosebush with dozens of large, clustered flowers, it is probably a *Floribunda* rose. Floribundas are not quite as big as the hybrid teas, but they produce many more blossoms. Gardeners often plant them in hedges, where they bloom all summer long. Floribunda bushes can be quite large, sometimes reaching seven feet tall.

For gardeners with limited space, there are miniature versions of the Floribundas. These scaled-down rosebushes grow only two feet tall, but they can produce dozens of small roses. The *China Doll* is a popular dwarf rose.

*Climbing* or *rambling* roses come in many colors and blossom types. Some produce large blossoms like those of the hybrid teas. Other climbers produce clusters of blossoms like the Floribundas. Many wild roses are natural climbers, their long stems weaving in and out of thickets or hedges.

Gardeners often use climbers to decorate fences or trellises. Although they look like vines, these roses can't climb on their own like a true vine. Their long, reaching stems must be tied to a trellis.

Among the largest of roses, *hybrid perpetuals* were the most popular hybrids in the 1800s. Before the hybrid perpetuals were developed, most roses would bloom for only a few weeks during the summer. The hybrid perpetuals bloomed all summer long. Some varieties grew blossoms seven inches across, with each flower producing as many as 100 petals.

In today's gardens the hybrid perpetuals have been largely replaced by newer hybrids. However, they are still grown in northern climates, where their hardiness helps them survive cold winters.

The wild rose, with its small blossoms, does not look much like the spectacular hybrids grown today. But a closer look reveals the same thorny stems, the same saw-toothed leaves, and the same nose-tingling aroma. Our modern hybrid roses may be bigger and more colorful than their wild ancestors. They may have fancier and longer names. But as William Shakespeare said,

*What's in a name?*
*That which we call a rose*
*by any other name*
*would smell as sweet.*

# INDEX

attar, 16
blossoms, 10, 15, 20, 23, 26, 29-30
bud, 20
bush, 20
China Doll, 25
Cleopatra, 6
climbers, 20, 26
Damask rose, 16
dwarf rose, 25
fertilize, 12
Floribunda, 23, 25-26
fossils, 9
fragrance, 9, 15, 30
fruit, 10
gardeners, 12, 23, 25-26
graft, 20
hedges, 9, 23, 26
hybrids, 12, 15, 29-30
jelly, 10
leaves, 30
perfume, 16, 19
petals, 6, 9-10, 19, 29
pollen, 12
rambling roses, 26
roots, 20
Rosa rugosa, 10
rose hips, 10
rosebush, 20, 23, 25
seeds, 12
Shakespeare, 30
stems, 15, 26, 30
tea, 10
vitamins, 10
wild roses, 9, 26, 30

**Photo Research**
Kristee Flynn

**Photo Credits**
COMSTOCK/Phylis Greenberg: cover
COMSTOCK/Art Gingert: 2
Ron Kimball: 4
COMSTOCK/COMSTOCK: 7
Robert & Linda Mitchell: 8, 13, 31
COMSTOCK/Michael Thompson: 11, 14, 18, 24, 27, 28
PHOTO RESEARCHERS, INC./Alan L. Detrick: 17
COMSTOCK/Russ Kinne: 21
Walt Anderson: 22

Text Copyright © 1996 by The Child's World®, Inc.
All rights reserved. No part of this book may be reproduced or utilized in any form or by any means without written permission from the publisher.
Printed in the United States of America.

Library of Congress Cataloging-in-Publication Data
Murray, Peter, 1952 Sept. 29-
Roses / by Peter Murray.
p. cm.
Includes Index.
ISBN 1-56766-192-0

1. Roses--Juvenile literature.   [1. Roses.]   I. Title.
QK495.R78M87   1995                              95-1747
583'.372--dc20